Map Scraps

Written by Alice Hemming

Illustrated by Alan Rowe

Collins

Stan and Fran seek the Chest of Hook Bill.

Look! A map is stuck in the sand.

The parrots flap.

The Chest
Hook Bill.

They grab and yank the map.
It splits.

Stan turns and sprints.

Fran scampers.

Stan and Fran are not as clever as parrots.

Stan and Fran dig. Wood splits.

The lid lifts. Objects glint.

The parrots lift the chest.

The map

The Chest of Hook Bill.

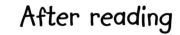

Letters and Sounds: Phase 4

Word count: 100

Focus on adjacent consonants with short vowel phonemes, e.g. /s/ /p/ /r/ /i/ /n/ /t/ /s/

Common exception words: of, the, to, they, are, there, so

Curriculum links (EYFS): Understanding the World

Curriculum links (National Curriculum, Year 1): Geography: Geographical skills and fieldwork

Early learning goals: Understanding: answer "how" and "why" questions in response to stories or events; Reading: use phonic knowledge to decode regular words and read them aloud accurately, read some common irregular words

National Curriculum learning objectives: Reading/word reading: read aloud accurately books that are consistent with their developing phonic knowledge and that do not require them to use other strategies to work out words; Reading/comprehension: develop pleasure in reading, motivation to read, vocabulary and understanding; make inferences on the basis of what is being said and done.

Developing fluency

- Your child may enjoy hearing you read the book.
- As you read, ask your child to read the speech bubbles with appropriate expression.

Phonic practice

- Practise reading words that contain adjacent consonants. Model sound talking the following word, saying each of the sounds quickly and clearly, e.g. g/r/a/b. Then blend the sounds together: **grab**.
- Ask your child to sound talk and blend the words **scampers**, **sprints** and **glint**.

Extending vocabulary

- Ask your child if they can think of an antonym (opposite) for each of the following words:

  clever (e.g. *stupid*)   stuck (e.g. *free*)   splits (e.g. *mends*)   hidden (e.g. *seen*)